TRIALS

Book of Poems

Brittani Nechelle Darensbourg

Brittani Nechelle Darensbourg
Trials

Published by Spines
ISBN 979-8-89950-215-6

Table of Contents

Isiah 43:2

"When thou passest through the waters; I will be with thee; and through the rivers, they shall not overflow thee: when thou walkest through the fire, thou shalt not be burned; neither shall the flame kindle upon thee."

Book Introduction

"In life, we all go through difficult times, facing trials and tribulations daily not knowing what to do. My very first Christian poetry collection informs readers that you can always depend on Jesus and his word, he will keep you in perfect peace when life gets hard."

-Brittani Darensbourg

-Author

Introduction / About the Author

"My Passion for poetry began when I was just 9 years old. I inspired others by being blessed with this gift from God at a young age. I won first place in the young Authors contest at Carver Elementary School in Hahnville, LA when I wrote my first book of poems ever. I'm blessed to present my third poetry book to poetry lovers and readers all around the world."

-Brittani Darensbourg

-Author

Anxiety

During the night, up with racing thoughts. Don't know what's gonna happen next. My spirit is very vexed. Going through this situation I didn't expect. Thinking of a negative turn out in my mind is a major effect. The outcome God gives me, I must respect. Chosen isolation from society, cause of built up anxiety.

-Brittani Darensbourg

Anxious

Difficult to focus on whats present. From the World, I'm absent. Being uneased for the rest of my life, is not my intent. Extremely nervous every day is wasted time spent. Growing impatient and eager, making it hard to be a believer. In a mindset of thankless and very anxious.

-Brittani Darensbourg

Depression

Days full of unhappiness and nights are very restless. In me, there's no peace. All hope left inside has decrease. No clue of where to turn or what to do. This is the hardest trial in life to go through. For a long time I've had it rough. Effort to ignore hurtful thoughts is not enough. Heart full of sadness and aggression, severe signs of.......... depression.

-Brittani Darensbourg

Weary

My existence is so dark, I'm confused on where to start and falling apart. Living life right yet still my days aren't looking so bright. Nothing else left to do, this season is getting harder to go through. My faith and strength is running low dearly. Currently in a phase of being weary.

-Brittani Darensbourg

Upset

Mentally disturbed
In a state of being perturb
Emotional distress not feeling the best
Hard for me to rest, need to worry less
Yet, I remain upset.

-Brittani Darensbourg

In Danger

In a place of suffering and possible harm
In denial of being warn
Put my life at a deadly risk
Listening to my heart, I wish
Stuck in a difficult place leaves me in anger
Lodged in great danger.

-Brittani Darensbourg

Addiction

My dependence is so strong
Don't know if this gonna last or how long
Trying to escape reality as of living a lie
Desperate to erase the painful memories
In my own world and mind I choose to hide
A bad habit that's hard to break
I need to be brave and cut the crave
Needed accomplishments are a restriction
Because of......Addiction.

-Brittani Darensbourg

Discouraged

Many goals I have set in life
The challenges cut deep as a knife
A spirit of heaviness that wears me down
In my tears, I drown
Upon my face I wear a frown
Lost all confidence
Result in negative consequence
Many try to encourage
But I remain ....discouraged.

-Brittani Darensbourg

Rejection

Never was approved

Always been refused

In a world where it's hard to be valued

But only misused and abused

On no occasion I was accepted, constantly ....Rejected.

-Brittani Darensbourg

Spiritual Warfare Of The Mind

Severely suffer from evil and unwanted thoughts. A clear eased mind can't be bought. A battle of conception that's hard to win. This line of thinking is pure sin. In desperate need of wanting my mind free, Negative and awful reasoning trying to take over me. Words to express this tribulation is hard to find. Fighting spiritual warfare of the mind.

-Brittani Darensbourg

Lack of Faith

I try to believe when it's hard to see. Circumstances I'm currently facing, it's hard for me to beat. The mountains are very high and the valleys are low. Don't know which way to go. Full of incredulity causes me to think foolishly. Don't know in the end, will I win. Every positive thought I deny before looking to the sky. Giving up during the wait, because of my lack of faith.

-Brittani Darensbourg

Unhappy

No joy consumed in me

Dissatisfied with life, no peace I see

Decision I made, leaves me very unpleased

Showing the world I'm discontent

Miserable in a situation that wasn't meant

Feeling very crappy, in a state of being unhappy.

-Brittani Darensbourg

Pain

Very distress, not depressed

Craving deeply for peace and joy, nothing less

Full of heartbreak, so much hurt I've intake

Going through a storm of emotional stress,
when will it break?

Extremely drain with so much pain.

-Brittani Darensbourg

Lost

Always made bad decisions, ending with horrible results. Hard to face the world and all the insults. Don't know where to go or who to turn to. Failure after failure, what should I do? Low self-esteem that shatters amazing dreams. Not believing in myself is a big cost, being very lost.

-Brittani Darensbourg

Lonely

Purely isolated

Being social is fairly complicated

Spending time alone keeps me motivated

Surrounded in the public eye has completely faded

Effortless reaching out to the world is oldly

I remain lonely.

-Brittani Darensbourg

Doubt

Hard to believe in a dream thats seems impossible to achieve. Is this meant for me? I always wonder. My emotional state goes back and forth. A positive and bright mindset needs to be force. Strong lack of conviction, with courage that's unreal as fiction. Leading myself down a route full of .....doubt.

-Brittani Darensbourg

Hurt

In this world with a heavy heart. Feels like life
is just falling apart. I'm broken, bruised, and
consider myself disused. A spirit full of pain,
happiness in the end is what I wanna gain.
It's possible to mend a broken heart, healing
is where I start. Some days I wish I can revert.
Eager to get away from all the hurt.

-Brittani Darensbourg

Failure

Tried and tried many of times, can't get ahead. Down a difficult path is where I always been led. Took different actions, however, entertained the same distractions, ending with no satisfaction. Having to start all over again but don't know where to begin. Wrong behavior causes such failure.

-Brittani Darensbourg

Weak

I can't go on like this any longer. Before I was a lot more stronger. Everything around me is telling me to give up. Trying my best to hang on. Every ounce of power on me is gone. No strength to keep going, In need of positivity for major growing. This game called life is hard to beat. All hope is lost when the spirit is very ......weak.

-Brittani Darensbourg

Stress

Difficult situation makes me worry, hard to focus, my mind is completely blurry. Mental state full of tension, a circumstance that has all of my attention. An emotional battle that's hard to win. Trying to hide a broken heart with a forgery grin. Uninterested in life, feeling very unalive. Withdrawn from rest, living with a lot of stress.

-Brittani Darensbourg

Bible Verses For Anxiety

Peter 5:7 *"Cast all your anxiety upon him; for he careth for you."*

Psalm 94:19 *"In the multitude of my thoughts within me thy comforts delight my soul."*

Bible Verses For Anxious

Philippians 4:6 *"Do not be anxious about anything, but in everything by prayer and supplication, with thanksgiving let your requests be made known to God."*

Philippians 4:7 *"And the peace of God, which passeth all understanding shall keep your hearts and minds through Christ Jesus."*

Bible Verse For Depression

Matthew 11:28 *"Come unto me, all ye that labor and are heavy laden, and I will give you rest."*

Bible Verse For Being Weary

Galatians 6:9 *"And let us not be weary in well doing; for in due season we shall reap, if we faint not."*

Bible Verse For Being Upset

James 1:19 *"Wherefore, my beloved brethren, let every man be swift to hear, slow to speak, slow to wrath."*

Bible Verse For Being In Danger

Psalms 81:7 *"Thou calledst in trouble and I delivered thee; I answered thee in the secret place of thunder: I proved thee at the waters of meribah. Selah."*

Bible Verses For Addiction

***Proverbs 20:1** "Wine is a mocker, strong drink is raging: and whosoever is deceived thereby is not wise."*

***1Corinthians 15:33** "Do not be deceived: Bad company ruins good morals."*

***1 Corinthians 10:13** "There hath no temptation taken you buy such as is common to man: But god is faithful, who will not suffer you to be tempted above that ye are able; but will with the temptation also make a way to escape, that ye may be able to bear it."*

Bible Verses For Being Discouraged

Joshua 1:9 *"Be strong and of a good courage. Have not I commanded thee? Be not afraid, neither be thou dismayed: for the Lord thy God is with thee whithersoever thou goest."*

Psalms 34:18 *"The Lord is nigh unto them that are of a broken heart; and saveth such as be a contrite spirit."*

Bible Verse For Rejection

John 15:18 *"If the world hate you, ye know that it hated me before it hated you."*

Bible Verses For Spiritual Warfare Of the Mind

2Corinthians 10:3-4 *"For though we walk in the flesh, we do not war after the flesh:"*

(For the weapons of our warfare are not carnal, but mighty through god to the pulling down of strong holds;)

Ephesians 6:11-12 *"Put on the whole armour of God, that ye may be able to stand against the wiles of the devil."*

For we wrestle not against flesh and blood, but against principalities, against powers, against the rulers of the darkness of this world, against spiritual wickedness in high places.

Isaiah 26:3 *"Thou wilt keep him in benefit peace, whose mind is stayed on thee. Because he trusteth in thee."*

Bible Verse For Lack of Faith

Hebrews 11:6 *"But without faith it is impossible to please him: for he that cometh to God must believe that he is and that he is a rewarder of them that diligently seek him."*

Bible Verse For Being Unhappy

Psalms 51:12 *"Restore unto me the joy of thy salvation; and uphold me with thy free spirit."*

Bible Verse For Pain

John 16:33 *"These things I have spoken unto you, that in me ye might have peace. In the world ye shall have tribulation: but be of good cheer; I have overcome the world."*

Bible Verse For Being Lost

Isaiah 41:10 *"Fear thou not; for I am with thee: be not dismayed; for I am thy God; I will strengthen thee; yea, I will help; yea, I will uphold thee with the right hand of my righteousness."*

Bible Verse For Being Lonely

Matthew 28:20 *"Teaching them to observe all things whatsoever I have commanded you; and, lo, I am with you always, even unto the end of the world. Amen."*

Bible Verse For Doubt

Matther 7:7-8 *"Ask and it shall be given to you; seek, and ye shall find; knock and it shall be opened to you:*

For everyone that asketh recieveth; and he that seeketh findeth; and to him that knocketh it shall be opened."

Bible Verse For Being Hurt

Jeremiah 29:11 *"I say this because I know what I am planning for you, "says the Lord." I have good plans for you, not plans to hurt. I will give you hope and a good future."*

Bible Verse For Failure

Psalms 37:24 *"Though he fall, he shall not be utterly cast down; for the Lord upholdeth him with his hand."*

Bible Verse For The Weak

Isaiah 40:31 *"But they who wait for the lord shall renew their strength, they shall mount up with wings like eagles; they shall run and not be weary; they shall walk and not faint."*

Bible Verse For Stress

James 1:2-3 "My brethren, count it all joy when ye fall into divers temptation;

"Knowing this that the trying of your faith worketh patience."

Also By
Brittani Nechelle Darensbourg

Trials: *Book of Poems -2025*
Mixed Emotions: *Book of Poems -2025*
Love, Passion, and Betrayal: *Book of Poems -2025*

Made in the USA
Columbia, SC
01 August 2025